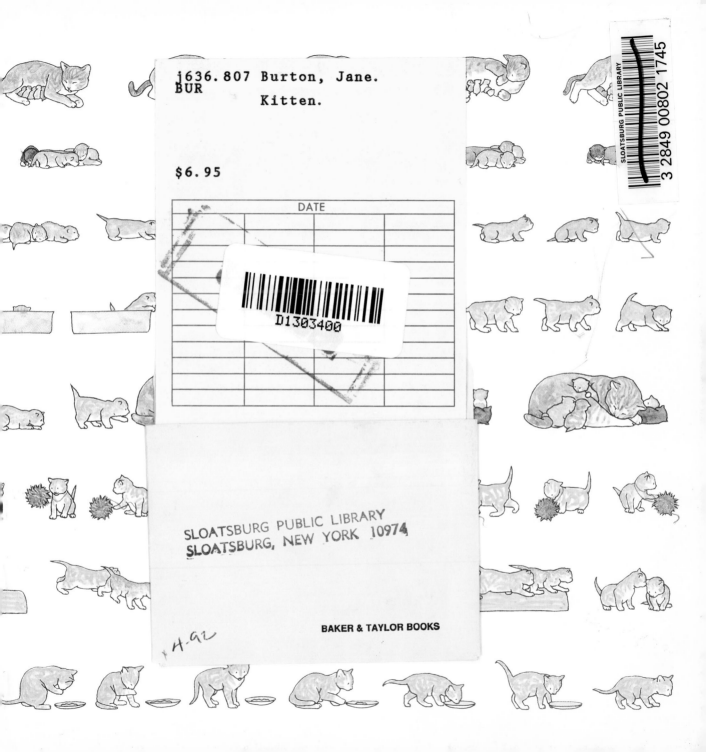

CREATED BY DORLING KINDERSLEY

Copyright © 1991 Dorling Kindersley Limited, London

All rights reserved.

Library of Congress Cataloging-in-Publication Data

Burton, Jane.
  Kitten/photographed by Jane Burton.—1st American ed.
  p. cm.—(See how they grow)
  Summary: Photographs and text show the development of a kitten from
birth to ten weeks old.
  ISBN 0-525-67343-1
  1. Kittens—Juvenile literature. 2. Cats—Development—Juvenile
literature. [1. Cats. 2. Animals—Infancy.] I. Title.
  II. Series.
  SF445.7.B874 1991
  636.8'07—dc20   90-43263
                                                              CIP
                                                               AC

First published in the United States in 1991 by Lodestar Books,
an affiliate of Dutton Children's Books, a division of
Penguin Books USA Inc.

Originally published in Great Britain in 1991 by
Dorling Kindersley Limited, 9 Henrietta Street, London WC2E 8PS

Printed in Italy by L.E.G.O.   ISBN 0-525-67343-1
First American Edition   10 9 8 7 6 5 4 3 2 1

Written and edited by Angela Royston
Art Editor Nigel Hazle
Illustrator Rowan Clifford
Jane Burton was assisted by Hazel Taylor

Typesetting by Goodfellow & Egan
Color reproduction by Scantrans, Singapore

SEE HOW THEY GROW
KITTEN

photographed by
JANE BURTON

Lodestar Books • Dutton • New York

Newborn

I have just been born.
I am still wet, and I
cannot see or hear.

My mother soon licks me dry.

This is
me

My mother feeds my brother
and sisters while I rest.

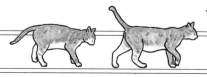

Cuddling

I am four days old.
I crawl over to my
brother and sisters.

I climb on top of
them, and we all sleep
together.

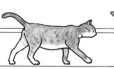

Now we are awake. My mother is cleaning herself while we try to feed.

Lost and alone

Now I am two weeks old.
I can see and hear, and today
I am going for a crawl
on my own.

I sniff the floor
as I crawl along.

Suddenly I miss my
mother. I mew loudly
until she comes to get me.

Exploring

Now I am four weeks old, and I am really ready to explore.

But what is this? I can see a dog over there.

I am hurrying back to my mother
and brother and sisters. Soon I
will be safe again.

I hope that dog goes away.

Playing

I am six weeks old,
and I love to romp
and play.

This is my yarn toy,
but the wool keeps
getting around
my neck!

14

That's better.
Now I'm free
again. I'll go
and play with
my ball.

15

Play fights

Won't anyone play with me today? I'll wait.

I am eight weeks old and getting really big now.

Here comes my brother.
I pounce on him, and
we roll on the
floor.

Looking after myself

I am ten weeks old
and nearly
grown up.

When I feel
hungry, I eat
from my saucer.

Now I am cleaning myself. I lick my paw and rub it on my face.

I lick myself all over.

19

See how I grew

One day old

Four days old

Two weeks old

Four weeks old

Six weeks old

  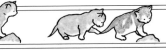  

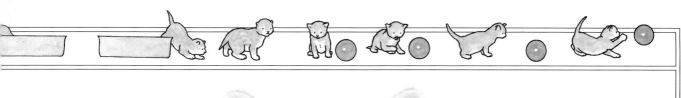

Eight weeks old

Ten weeks old